I Love You So Much

I Love You So Much

Carl Norac ♥ Illustrated by Claude K. Dubois

SCHOLASTIC INC.

**NewYork Toronto London Auckland Sydney
Mexico City   New Delhi   Hong Kong**

This morning when Lola woke up,
she felt something special on the tip of her tongue.

I know the words are there, she said to herself.
I can feel them puffing out my cheeks.

Lola wanted to say her special words to Daddy.
But it was too late. He was already leaving for work.

Lola wanted to say her special words to Mommy.
But Mommy was very busy.

"Mommy, I want to tell you . . . ," Lola whispered.
"Can it wait, angel?" said Mommy. "You'll be late for school."

On the school bus, it was much too
noisy for Lola to say her special words.

At the playground, Lola walked up to her teacher.
But her teacher was already holding another child.

In class, Lola looked over at the annoying boy next to her.
I won't tell him *my special words,* she thought.

At lunchtime, in the cafeteria, everybody was chewing and chomping. Lola kept quiet. Special words should not be chomped, she decided.

During recess, all the children played running games.
Lola didn't say a single word, *especially* not a special word.

After school, Lola saw Frankie, the Skateboard King. Lola smiled.
She decided to say her special words to him.

But *Zoom!* The rat sped past Lola without stopping, without waiting to hear her special words.

Back on the bus, it was too noisy again. Lola felt sulky now.

At home, in the living room, Lola sulked some more.

Even when her parents got home, Lola kept sulking.

She didn't feel like saying her special words anymore.

During supper, the meat felt hard,
the salad felt mushy, and the lemonade was sour.

"What's wrong, Lola?" Mommy asked.
"Won't you tell us?" Daddy asked.

Lola thought long and hard. *I won't say anything,* she thought.
Nobody cares. I won't say my special words.

But her cheeks started puffing up, bigger and bigger and bigger still.
Suddenly Lola shouted:

"Mommy, Daddy, I love you, I love you! I love you so much!"

Finally Lola had said her special words.
The words came flying out of her mouth and worked their magic.
Instantly Mommy and Daddy hugged their Lola and kissed her cheeks.

As she went upstairs to bed, Lola felt a little nervous.
What if the special words don't come back tomorrow? she worried.

But as soon as Lola turned off her light and snuggled into bed, she felt happy. Tomorrow's special words were already on the tip of her tongue.

For Antoine   For Ysé   *Merci, Sarah and Erica Moroz*
—C.N.   —C.K.D.   —BDD

ISBN 0-439-18730-3

Copyright © 1996 by *l'école des loisirs*, Paris.
English translation by Delphine Simone copyright © 1998 by Bantam Doubleday Dell Publishing Group, Inc.
All rights reserved. Published by Scholastic Inc., 555 Broadway, New York, NY 10012,
by arrangement with Doubleday, a division of Bantam Doubleday Dell Publishing Group, Inc.
SCHOLASTIC and associated logos are trademarks and/or registered trademarks of Scholastic Inc.

12 11 10 9 8 7 6   0 1 2 3 4 5/0

Printed in the U.S.A.   08

First Scholastic Book Clubs paperback printing, September 2000

The text of this book is set in 16-point Gill Sans.
Book design by Trish Parcell Watts